About the Author

Charlotte Sebag-Montefiore's third book, is a new departure for her into the fascinating world of dinosaurs. Charlotte says that her interest in dinosaurs springs from what they have in common with us, - for some were bipeds, and the fate of all hinged on climate change.

About the Illustrator

Anita is an illustrator based in northern Germany. With her family she lives in a small town by the sea. All her inspiration comes from this environment. After studying designs and working in the advertising industry, she got back to her life-long passion for drawing and illustrating.

With best wishes from
Charlotte Sebag-Montefiore

Herbie and the T. Rex

Charlotte Sebag-Montefiore

Herbie and the T. Rex

Olympia Publishers
London

www.olympiapublishers.com
OLYMPIA PAPERBACK EDITION

A CIP catalogue record for this title is available from the British Library.

ISBN: 978-1-78830-497-9

First Published in 2020

Olympia Publishers
Tallis House
2 Tallis Street
London
EC4Y 0AB

Printed in Great Britain

Dedication

This book is dedicated to my grandchildren, Lily, Hannah, Flora and Moshe.

Acknowledgements

I would like to acknowledge the support of my husband, and also of Chantelle Wadsworth.

We used to live everywhere, even in your country 220 million years ago, or was it 224 million years ago? No-one really knows and it doesn't make much difference, does it? We can agree it was a very long time ago.

I am Herbie the Herbivore. I think we are the oldest dinosaurs of all and very important. Perhaps without us there wouldn't be any other dinosaurs! Meet my pop. He is a good jumper, although he often jumps the wrong way. He is not very clever. Most dinosaurs aren't clever.

Take my friend, Dippy. He's enormous, but he spends so much time sending messages to his tail that he doesn't have much time for anything else!

He often tells me about his family problems. They all have to turn around at the same time or they whack each other with their tails! He has another big problem, the monstrous T. Rex... Of course, we're all afraid of them. But Dippy has his own difficulties.

If a T. Rex chases Dippy, he can't zigzag as his huge tail throws him off balance.

Let's meet my brother Spiky! He is not really
my brother, but my mum likes him and he lives
with us. He has spikes along his crest. He thinks it
makes him look smarter than the rest of us, but
it's wishful thinking on his part. His best friend is
Stegs the stegosaurus. He's as big as a bus!

Now let's meet Spiny: she is my friend. Spiny has a very useful feature. She has spines round her mouth which change colour depending on which way she is going. She's a lot like me, we are both clever!

I am older than Spiky and Spiny, so I try to look after them. One day I took them out to play.

I called Dippy. "Give us a ride, Dippy. Bend down and we'll jump on your neck." Dippy has a very, very long neck and if he bends all the way down, we can jump right up quite easily. Spiky put his arms round her waist and we all hung on as tight as we could!

Then Dippy lifted up his neck like the big dippers that you have and we all screamed! It's great up there, you can see for miles. And off we went. Although he is so big, and we are so small, we like the same leaves.

"Take us to the tasty tree, Dippy, where we went last time," I said. Dippy loped along at quite a pace, and we were there in no time!

We can't reach the best leaves without Dippy. You see, the best and sweetest leaves are at the very top of the tree. It's not fair on us short herbivores really, but that's the way it is!

When Dippy s t r e t c h e d his neck: we all had to be careful not to fall. I looked around from time to time as we ate the yummy leaves. I didn't want a nasty surprise.

It was a lovely view up there. Hills and plains, grass and herbivores grazing peacefully as far as the eye could see. Still, I kept a lookout - you never know!

Then I saw it, the biggest T. Rex ever!
"Careful, Dippy," I said, not wanting to frighten him.

"It's time to stop eating now."
Dippy always listened to me.
"Now Dippy, stay exactly where you
are. Whatever you do, don't run. When
I say wave your tail, wave it, OK?"

"OK," Dippy replied. "But what is this all about? Is it a new game?"

"Yes," I said. "It's a great new game. I'll tell you the rules later. But you must do exactly what I say."

I then turned to Spiky and Spiny. "You two, just hang on!" I turned around slowly, terrified to look back at the T. Rex. They have such huge mouths, terrifying teeth and scary arms to grab you!

The T. Rex was close. It couldn't understand why we didn't run away. Its horrid little arms clawed at the empty air.

"Wave your tail now, Dippy," I SHOUTED. He did as he was told and waved his tail knocking the T. Rex's legs from under him.

"Don't turn round, Dippy," I shouted. "Just stay there." The T. Rex wasn't used to being knocked over. It hit its head on a sharp rock as it fell to the ground and just lay there. Would it get up?

After several goes, the T. Rex managed to get up, but it looked shaken as it stood still, watching us. "Wave your tail again, Dippy," I shouted. Dippy waved his tail and knocked the huge T. Rex over once again. This time it didn't hit its head, but its legs went up in the air helpless, like a tortoise upside down. When he finally managed to get up, he scowled at Dippy, turned and limped off.

I watched him until I was sure he wasn't going to come back. "Dippy," I said, "you're a great Diplodocus. You are absolutely herborific! This wasn't a game. You just defeated a T. Rex!" Dippy looked proud as Spiny, Spiky and I cheered and cheered!!!

Other Books by
Charlotte Sebag-Montefiore

Who am I?
A Book of Riddles
(2016)
ISBN:
978-1-84897-744-0

Who am I? More
Animal Riddles
(2018)
ISBN:
978-1-78830-060-5